D0175059

Young children are fascinated by zoos and safari parks.

To see a huge elephant or a long-necked giraffe in real life brings alive the pictures they see in books.

Zoos today carry out a lot of scientific research. They also protect endangered species by breeding animals in captivity. Some of these animals can then be returned to their own habitat to live and breed again in the wild.

British Library Cataloguing in Publication Data
Gagg, M. E.
    The Zoo.
    I. Title   II. Breeze, Lynn   III. Series
    590'.74'4
    ISBN 0-7214-1175-4

First edition

Published by Ladybird Books Ltd Loughborough Leicestershire UK
Ladybird Books Inc Auburn Maine 04210 USA
Printed in England

The Zoo

by M. E. GAGG
illustrated by LYNN BREEZE

Ladybird Books

Let's go to the zoo.

Here are the lions.
The cubs are playing.

This is a tiger.

How many cubs
are there?

Look at the
chimpanzees
climbing and
swinging.

Here are the elephants.

They like to play with
water.

Look at the giraffe drinking water.

Giraffes have very long necks.

These are
kangaroos.
Where is the
baby?

Look at the
polar bears.

They like to swim.

Here are the seals.
They like fish for dinner.

Here are the penguins.

This is a big fat
hippopotamus.

She has a baby.

The parrots have lovely feathers.

How many other birds can you count?

And last of all is
the panda.
What is he eating?

Did you enjoy the zoo?